Trafalgar Bear

Jenny Stevens

Published by

 Melrose Books

An Imprint of Melrose Press Limited
St Thomas Place, Ely
Cambridgeshire
CB7 4GG, UK
www.melrosebooks.co.uk

FIRST EDITION

Copyright © Jenny Stevens 2018

The Author asserts her moral right to
be identified as the author of this work

Cover and illustrations by Elly Eveleigh

ISBN   978-1-912640-12-6 Paperback
**   978-1-912640-13-3 ePub**
**   978-1-912640-14-0 Mobi**

Printed and bound in Great Britain by:
Print & Sign Centres Ltd
480 Gorgie Road
Edinburgh
EH11 2RZ

The Stevens family were getting ready for a day trip to London, everyone was dressed in their best clothes, even Bear had a new coat to wear and he looked very smart.

"Come on, Jonathan," shouted Mum. "You must get your coat and shoes on please, or we will miss the train." Bear looked on smiling, he was very pleased to be going on the trip and Jonathan let him wear his new coat which was bright red and nice and warm.

On the way to the train station, everyone was smiling and happy, looking forward to visiting lots of interesting places that neither Jonathan nor bear had ever seen before.

Jonathan loved travelling by train, he always sat by the window looking out as the countryside rushed past. He could see horses, cows, sheep and houses.

Bear was sitting by the window, too. He was looking for other bears, of course he did not see any and that made him a little sad, but Jonathan had promised him he would meet some bears when they visited the zoo later.

When they arrived in London, it was very busy and noisy. Bear was not too sure he liked it very much, but Jonathan was holding him tight and Bear was feeling safe and excited.

"First stop, Trafalgar Square," said Daddy, "then we go to the Tower of London and then the zoo." They have bears at the zoo. Jonathan told Bear this and he was looking forward to meeting them.

"A busy day ahead," said Mummy, and Jonathan and Bear nodded their heads in agreement.

The ride on the tube train to Trafalgar Square was very hot and it was a tight squeeze to get into the train carriage, but they soon arrived and the sun shone in a clear blue sky, even though it was chilly as they came out of the tube station.

"At last," said Daddy. "Everyone hold hands and stay together."

Jonathan looked up at a large statue of a horse. A man was sitting on it wearing a funny hat. Everything looked big and exciting to Bear and Jonathan, so exciting that Jonathan forgot to hold onto Bear and he fell into a puddle. Jonathan was so mesmerised by the surroundings, he did not realise that Bear had gone.

Bear was very wet and realised that he was not with his family any more: he had been left behind, no sign of Jonathan or Mummy and Daddy. Bear was on his own, cold and scared.

Pedro the pigeon was flying very low. He was trying to dive-bomb the humans who were walking on the pavements. This was his favourite game and he spent lots of time playing it. He thought it was funny that the humans keep ducking and glaring at him.

Suddenly, Pedro heard a sound like sobbing. He looked down from his lofty position sitting on the Trafalgar Square horse's tail and he saw Bear. A soggy heap of bright red cloth huddled on the side of the road.

"Aye, aye," he said. "What is this I spy with my little eye?"

Swooping down, Pedro scooped Bear up in his bright red pigeon feet and carried him away over the rooftops of London town.

9

Having never flown before, Bear was not sure he liked the experience. They were going very fast, and to be honest, Pedro did smell rather strange. Not like Jonathan's mummy, who always smelt of vanilla and flowers.

Realising this was quite an adventure, Bear tried to enjoy it and by the time they had landed on Pedro's pigeon coop, Bear was smiling from ear to furry ear.

Bear was still quite wet and soggy, so Pedro hung his red coat out to dry on his owner's washing line. Bear was looking a little bedraggled and seemed upset and sad.

"What's your name?" Pedro asked Bear.

"Bear is my name."

"Mmm." A little puzzled, Pedro thought before saying, "Just Bear, not Bob Bear, Billy Bear or Edward Bear?"

"No, just Bear," said Bear.

"I am Pedro Pigeon. It is nice to meet you, Just Bear."

The two friends smiled at each other as they settled down for a rest in the pigeon coop while Bear's coat dried on the line. Bear did not have the best sleep he had ever had as he was balancing on a piece of wood, but he was so tired after his adventure flying high in the sky that he would have slept anywhere. Bear's red coat was dry and he put it on.

"Very smart," said Pedro. "I think that we should go and see some of the sights of London, why waste a smart red coat?"

London Zoo was first on Pedro's list. Bear was glad, because he wanted to meet some of his relatives that Jonathan had told him lived in the zoo and he thought maybe Jonathan would be there. Despite feeling excited about his adventure, Bear was a little sad. He missed Jonathan and his mummy and daddy and wondered if he would ever see them again.

London Zoo

After another fur-raising flight across London, Bear and Pedro arrived at London Zoo. Not the usual way into the zoo through the front gate, oh no, but flying over the fence and landing neatly on the grass.

Bear heard roars, rumbles and squeaks all around him, he shivered and wondered what the day would bring?

"First stop, the bears," said Pedro with a chuckle.

Polar bears. They were not interested in Bear, they really are the wrong colour fur, you know. They sniffed their displeasure and disappeared into the water.

Brown bears, that's more like it.

"They look more like you, Bear," said Pedro, smiling.

But, no, the brown bears were not interested in the little bear wearing the bright red coat. Pedro was sad, he thought he had found Bear's forever home.

Well, while we are here, we might as well look around. How about the Penguins, waddling and chatting together. They made Bear smile.

Then the lions and tigers prowling around their cages sniffing the air.

"These look like Jonathan's granny's cats, Ruby and Alfie, but they are much bigger," said Bear, and he suddenly felt homesick.

Bear looked closely through the bars at a large lion. The lion roared, "Hello," and nearly blew Bear over onto his bottom. "Time to go," said Pedro, and Bear agreed.

Tower of London

"Where are we going next?" asked Bear, politely.

"The Tower of London to meet my friend Rebel the raven," said Pedro.

Rebel is a lovely, black, shiny raven: a guardian of the Tower of London, and he was the boss. Rebel enjoyed telling Bear about his job, a very important job indeed.

"If the ravens ever leave the Tower, it will fall down."

Bear was impressed by Rebel's story.

"There are seven ravens at the tower and one called Paul is my best friend. We live next door to the Wakefield tower and are protected birds. Very important indeed." Rebel's chest puffed out.

Very regal, thought Bear.

"Don't you ever want to fly away?" asked Bear.

"Oh no, our wings are clipped and if we go away we get the sack. Raven George was dismissed from duties after eating TV aerials and he is now living in the East End. Such a sad end to an illustrious career," said Rebel, laughing.

They said their farewells and the two friends waved to Rebel and wandered off to find lunch.

Buckingham Palace

Hungry work, this sightseeing, thought Bear.

Pedro was picking up bits of food from the path. Bear, a little more fussy, demanded honey sandwiches. Now where can a pigeon and bear find such fine foods?

Wandering down the pathways, Bear was wondering about Jonathan and his family. Were they missing Bear? Would he ever see them again? Pedro, however, was more interested in making Bear's day in London an adventure, so the next stop was the house where the Queen lives, Buckingham Palace. Bear did not know what that meant.

The Queen, he wondered, puzzled. Who is that?

"The Queen is in charge of our country. She is royalty," said Pedro.

Buckingham Palace was huge, especially to a small bear wearing a red coat. Looking through the railings at the big house with lots of flags flying outside it.

Bear thought, "It is much bigger than my house. It would take Mummy and Daddy days to clean it."

They walked down Horse Guards Parade together.

There were men in uniform guarding the palace, standing in little boxes. Pedro told Bear they were soldiers. Wearing scarlet tunics they looked very smart.

"They wear Busbies on their heads made from bear skins," explained Pedro.

Bear looked alarmed and gulped, but Pedro said this was a 200-year-old tradition, something called history. Bear thought he would ask Jonathan about this when they were back together.

A guard with a bear skin hat winked at the two friends as they made their way down Horse Guards Parade avoiding the puddles left from the overnight rain.

"Sometimes the Queen rides her horse here," explained Pedro, "and all the tourists watch her."

Bear, not wanting to appear silly, just nodded his head. "Tourists," he thought. "What are they?" Something to find out about on another day.

Bear wished he had worn his wellingtons, his feet were getting a little soggy.

The sky was turning deep red, Pedro thought it was time he returned Bear to his family. Bear looked sad and Pedro knew he had to help him find Jonathan. Bear liked that idea and smiled at Pedro.

On the way back to Trafalgar Square, they met some of Pedro's street friends: a dog called Sunny, who belonged to a street entertainer …

… and a cat called Dunbar who lived in a pub: he was very old and wise.

Bear wanted to be back at home, sitting on Jonathan's bed while Jonathan read stories to him. Bear would have some exciting stories for Jonathan. He smiled to himself, imagining Jonathan's surprise at what he had seen today.

Pedro picked Bear up and flew quickly to Trafalgar Square, he sat him down on the back of a rather grand horse.

Pedro perched on the head of one of the golden lions who stand on guard at Trafalgar Square.

"Well, Bear," he said, "at least these lions won't roar at you."

Bear smiled at his joke.

A few minutes later, Jonathan and Mummy and Daddy came round the corner. They looked tired and upset, but as soon as they saw the little bear in the bright red coat they ran to him. Jonathan picked Bear up in his arms and gave him a big cuddle.

"Oh, you silly bear. Where have you been? You have missed a lovely day in London."

Bear smiled to himself thinking, "If only you knew."

Pedro watched and chuckled, he would always remember this day. "My new friend, Bear," he thought, "should now be called Trafalgar Bear. After all his adventures, he was still smiling. A very brave bear indeed."

I wonder if they will meet again. Who knows what the future will bring for these two friends? Let's hope there are more adventures in store for them.

Pedro smiled his kind pigeon smile before taking off for home.